DISCARDED
From Nashville Public Library
D1247479

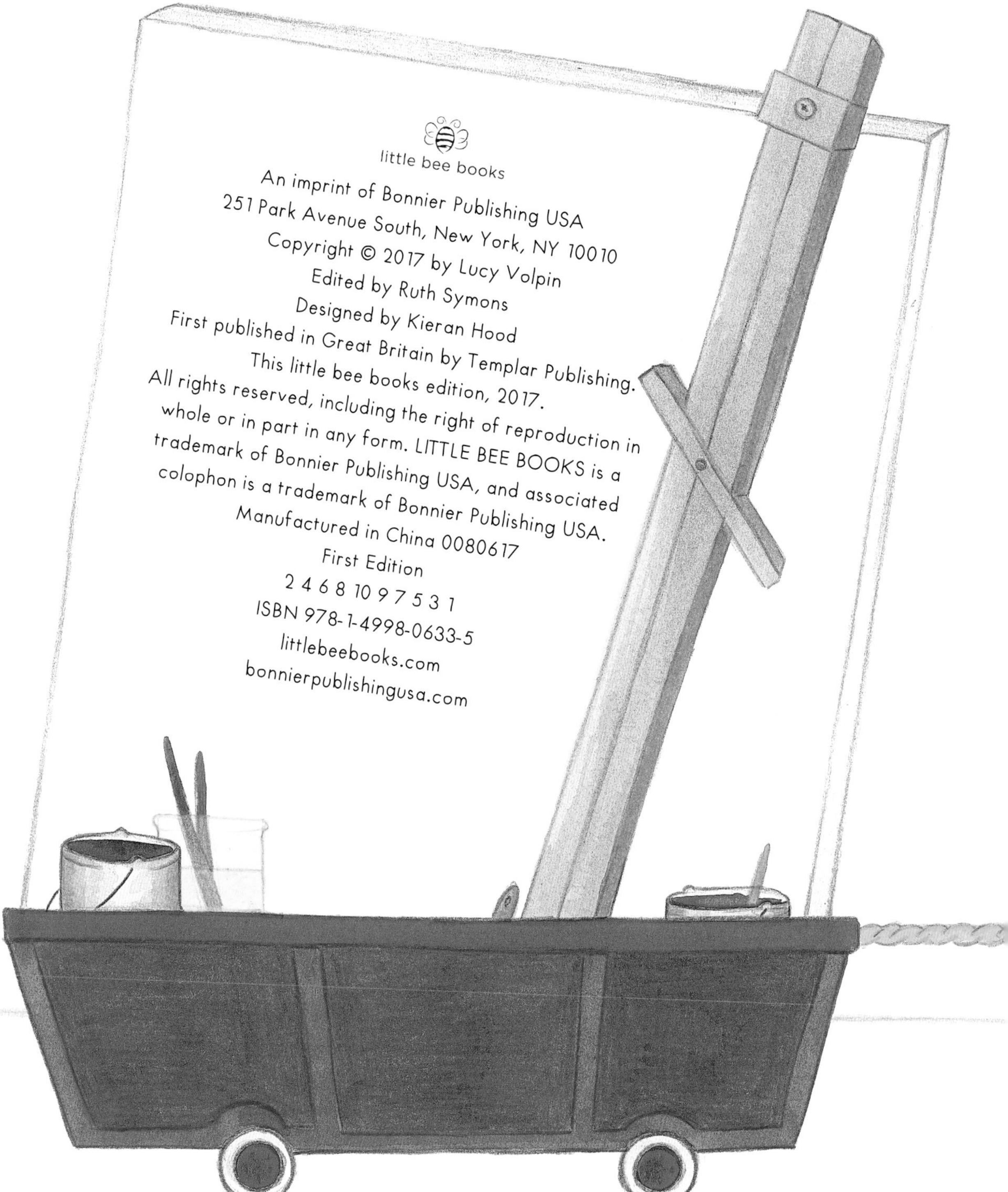

little bee books
An imprint of Bonnier Publishing USA
251 Park Avenue South, New York, NY 10010
Copyright © 2017 by Lucy Volpin
Edited by Ruth Symons
Designed by Kieran Hood
First published in Great Britain by Templar Publishing.
This little bee books edition, 2017.
All rights reserved, including the right of reproduction in whole or in part in any form. LITTLE BEE BOOKS is a trademark of Bonnier Publishing USA, and associated colophon is a trademark of Bonnier Publishing USA.
Manufactured in China 0080617
First Edition
2 4 6 8 10 9 7 5 3 1
ISBN 978-1-4998-0633-5
littlebeebooks.com
bonnierpublishingusa.com

Crocodali

Lucy Volpin

little bee books

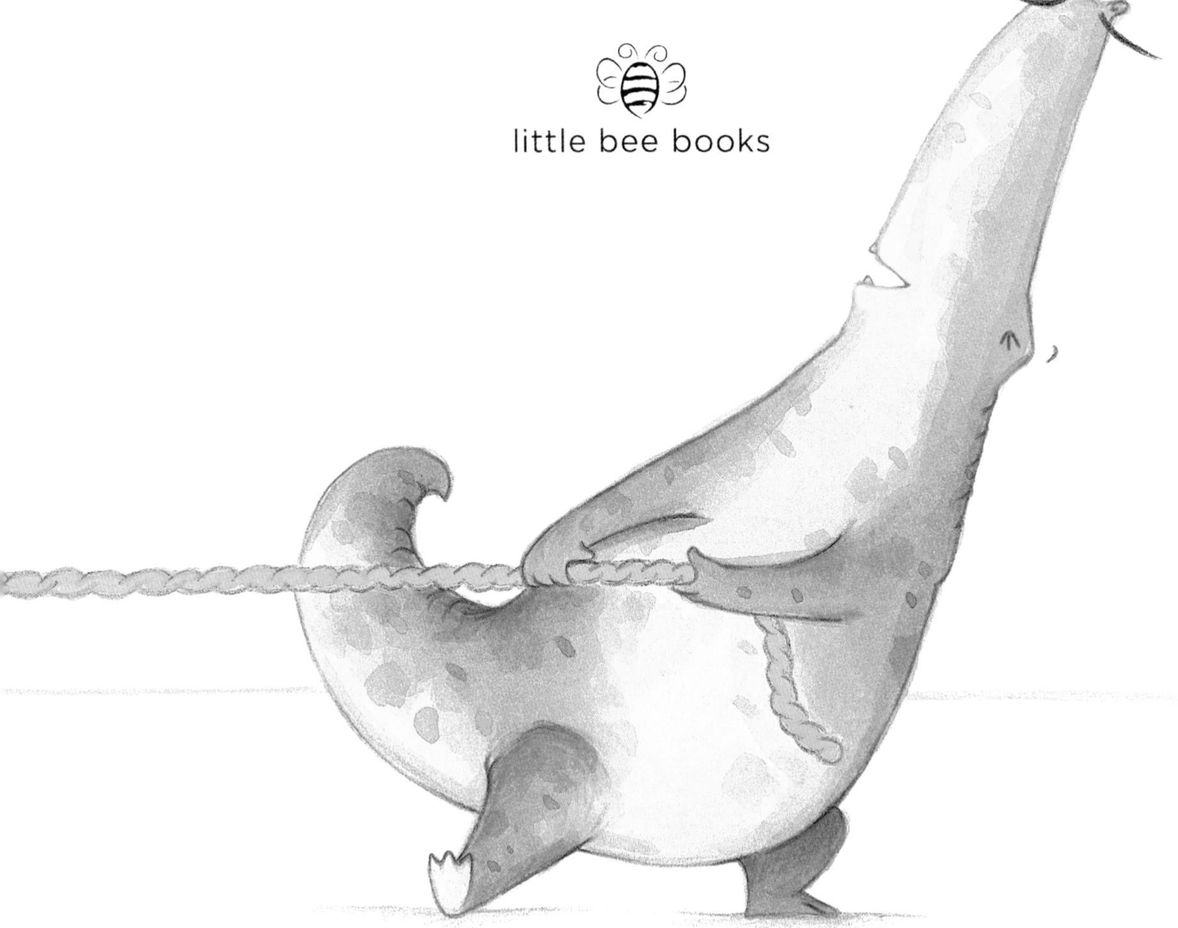

NASHVILLE PUBLIC LIBRARY

Do you mind? I'm very busy here.

I am Crocodali, the most talented painter in the whole wide world. And **you** are in **my** studio!

I'm sorry, I have no time for autographs today.
I am about to create a masterpiece. . . .

The thing is, I just can't quite get this canvas straight. Now that you're here, you might as well help.

Could you tilt the book to the right?

That should do it.

Oh no, you've tilted it **much** too far!
What am I going to do?

You'll have to tilt it to the left now.
Go on.

Just a little this time.

I said, "Just a little"!

This is a disaster.
My paints have gone everywhere!

You've done enough for today.
Just sit there and read while I clean up. . . .
And don't you **dare** move a thing!

Did you turn the page?
I knew I shouldn't have trusted you.
I'll have to start all over again.

But hang on . . . that looks quite nice.
Maybe you're onto something. . . .

Give the book a shake and see what happens.

NOT

SO

HARD!

Now the paint's all over me too!
I hope you're happy with yourself.

Let's get this place cleaned up.

Well, look at that. I think I like it.
But is it upside down?

I'll just turn it around and
add some finishing touches. . . .

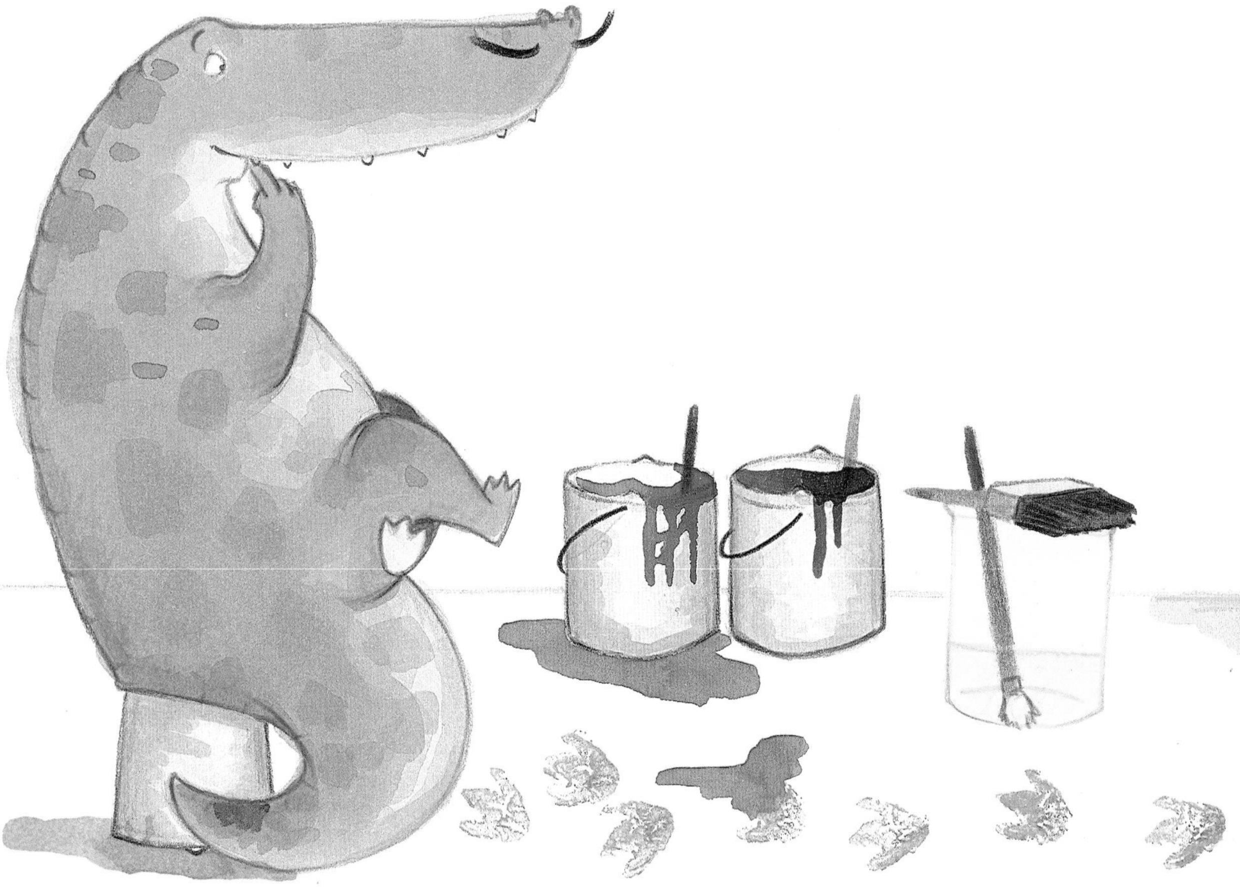

A dab of purple . . .

. . . some yellow, some red . . .

. . . and then mix it all up!

Would you help me out?
Go on—rub the canvas to
add the final touch.

It's a masterpiece! I really **am** the greatest painter in the world.

Now I'll put it over here to dry. But maybe we could speed things up a bit. Could you blow on the painting?

One, two, three . . .

BLOW!

Oh . . .

Let's start again!